For Kaylee, forever in our hearts. Our first
Cavalier King Charles Spaniel, whose snoring
kept us up at night but still sparked my passion
for this wonderful breed.

Cavie's Magical Wish

Cavie, a Cavalier King Charles Spaniel, bounced through the blooming meadow near his home on his way to visit friends.

As Cavie ran through a stream, he spied his friend Finley leaping over the large stones in the water. "Ha, ha! Try to catch me, Finley," Cavie called out while they chased each other in a game of tag.

While racing along the stream, Cavie saw another friend, Rory, hopping high in the air. Cavie laughed, "Let's play hopscotch on the rocks."

Cavie stepped on one of the rocks when he heard a chirp. Looking around he saw a hummingbird trapped in a spider's web, trying to break free. The tiny bird was pecking against the sticky spider maze with her beak, trying to get away.

With a quick swipe of his paw, Cavie tore through the web, freeing the hummingbird. The little bird flew out of the broken spider web and whistled happily, "You saved me! I'm free!" As the tiny bird soared around her new friends, she buzzed, "My name is Hummer and I'm happy to meet you all!"

Cavie chuckled, "Hi, Hummer. Come play with us!"

While playing, Hummer whispered to Cavie, "I have a secret to tell you. I have magical powers. Since you saved me from the spider's web, I can grant you one wish. What would you like it to be?"

Cavie thought, "Hmm. What should I wish for?

A big juicy bone?

New toys?

Or to fly in the sky like Hummer does?"

As Cavie dreamed about a wish, he remembered, "I used to be trapped like Hummer but in a different way. While Hummer had been caught in the spider's web for a short time, I was kept in a dog crate for several years at a puppy mill. I lived in a small cage and didn't get to play outside or have a family to take care of me."

Cavie continued, "I feel lucky to have been rescued last year by my new family.

I now have a soft bed, delicious food, and a kind family." Cavie recalled the other dogs he lived with at the puppy mill, "I hope my friends found a family to love them, too."

Cavie realized, "I know just what to do." He blurted out, "Hummer, I have thought of the perfect wish! I wish all my old friends still living at the puppy mill would get their wish: to find a forever home with a caring family."

Hummer was amazed. "What a wonderful wish! You want to give up your wish for all your old friends so they can get their own wish?"

"Yes!" Cavie shouted. "I'm so glad my family saved me that I want other dogs to have the same chance for a happy home."

Hummer beamed. "Your kindness is truly magical, Cavie." With a flick of her wing, Hummer chanted, "I now grant your wish. From this day forward, each of your puppy mill friends will get their wish to be adopted by a loving family."

Suddenly, Cavie and his friends watched as a shower of shining stars rained down from the sky, each holding a magical wish for each dog in need.

With a cheery tune, Hummer sang, "They are all going to find their forever home. You've given them the greatest wish of all."

Author Julie Huetsch shares her heart and home with two adorable Cavalier King Charles Spaniels, Granger and Sophie. Her love for this beautiful breed and her commitment to dog rescue inspired her to write the delightful children's book *Cavie's Magical Wish*, the first in her series, Cavie Tales™.

Granger has a touching rescue story. Saved from a puppy mill by The Cavalier Rescue, Granger joined Julie's family with a heart condition, hearing loss, and separation anxiety. With the love of his new family, Granger quickly adapted and now happily claims the title of king of their castle! Julie's other dog, Sophie, is on a special mission, training to be a touch therapy dog to bring joy to children in hospitals. This is a perfect role for sweet Sophie!

Julie is also passionate about giving back; a portion of the proceeds from her book sales goes directly to The Cavalier Rescue, helping dogs in need of rescue and rehabilitation.

Cavie Tales

cavietales.com™

Illustrator Siski Kalla has fostered 15 dogs in the past ten years, four of which were 'foster fails'. One of them, Osito, illustrated above, was even adopted by another family... but he cried so much, they asked Siski to take him back! She has never been happier to fail at something four times over!

Siski has illustrated more than 20 children's picture books, and quite a few of them are about dogs. Her most recent book, *Gertie is Not ALL Dogs*, published by Clavis Publishing, is available in English, Spanish and Dutch; and her book *A Shoe is to Chew: a dog's first book of definitions* is available in English.

Made in United States
Orlando, FL
30 October 2024

53196489R00018